ORC CHARMING

AVA ROSS

ENCHANTED STAR PRESS

ORC CHARMING

Love at First Orc Series, Book 0.5

Cover Art: Wolfraven Studio

Editing: JA Wren and Owl Eyes Proofs & Edits

*For my family who
always believe in me.*

SERIES BY AVA

Mail-Order Brides of Crakair
Brides of Driegon
Fated Mates of the Ferlaern Warriors
Fated Mates of the Xilan Warriors
Holiday with a Cu'zod Warrior
Galaxy Games
Alien Warrior Abandoned
Beastly Alien Boss
Bride of the Fae
A Sci-Fi Holiday Tail
Monsterville, USA
Monster on Board
(co-written with Alana Khan)
Love at First Orc
Monster Mate Hunt
Third Galaxy on the Left
You can find her books on Amazon.

ORC CHARMING

**I'm falling for my gorgeous orc roommate,
but he's got a secret.**

I'm serving up the morning crowd at my struggling diner when a tall, brooding, yet surprisingly endearing orc strolls in, making my heart flip like a pancake on the griddle. Could he be the butter to my syrup?

He eyes the menu like a kid in a candy store, and it tugs on my heartstrings. Is he down on his luck? I trust my gut and give him my breakfast special, a full meal for only ninety-nine cents. Next thing you know, I'm inviting Deegar to crash on my couch.

As a recent arrival from the orc kingdom, Deegar needs help settling so I give him a job at the diner and offer myself as his guide to all things human. We navigate thrift store misadventures (they seriously need orc-sized attire) and set up his social media presence. Yes, he's cute (actually, he's devastatingly handsome), but does he really need a fan club?

I'm falling head over heels for Deegar, and I hope he feels the same, but I can't help feeling he's hiding something from me.

Can our whirlwind romance survive the wildest of twists, or is our love fated for a tragic ending?

Orc Charming is set in the Love at First Orc Series. Expect an orc who's creative with his . . . (cough), size difference, only one bed, a hero with a secret, a curvy heroine, and plenty of spice and humor. HEA guaranteed.

Pick up the rest of the Love at First Orc Series!
Orc Charming
(Free with Newsletter Signup)
Orc-us Pocus
Orc-ishly Ever After
Tinsel & Tusks
Orc-wardly Yours
Gaming the Orc

Companion stories
Single Orc Dad
(part of the Sweet Monster Treats world)

CHAPTER 1

CAT

The smell of brewing coffee filled the air as I hustled around my little seaside diner, preparing for the breakfast crowd. Marge had settled in her usual spot near the front right window and was drenching her pancakes in maple syrup. And Dr. Yang sat alone at the bar, savoring his scrambled eggs and homestyle toast. They were regulars here, part of the heartbeat of Seashell Diner.

I wasn't sure what I would've done without them when Mom got sick and died. They'd stepped in—actually helping serve customers—and then stood at Mom's graveside beside me.

When the door chimed, I glanced up from where I wiped down the butcherblock counter my dad had built for mom so long ago. Sadly, he was gone, too. An accident claimed him when I was eight, while Mom passed just a year ago.

An orc entered the diner, his green skin still startling despite seeing them on the TV and around town for the past month. Six weeks ago, a delegation of orcs emerged from a mountain range and announced they wanted to form a treaty with us to join human society. After the initial treaty was formed, the first wave of orcs arrived, most of them males. Many of their women had died, and those joining humans hoped to find mates from among us.

I wasn't sure what I thought about all that, but each orc I met was super friendly and kind. They were an asset to our society.

On TV, I saw that a second delegation had arrived a few weeks ago to further relations with us, and I was curious to hear what they'd discuss.

The orc walked up to the counter and took a seat —perched on it, that is. Orcs stood over seven feet tall, and unless an establishment had big and tall chairs and booths, they had a hard time fitting. Fortunately, my stools could handle almost any sized butt.

I handed him a laminated menu. "Welcome to the Seashell Diner. Can I get you something to drink?"

"What do you recommend?" For whatever reason, his deep voice sent a thrill through me, making my heart flip.

"Most request coffee or tea at this time of day, but . . . Have you tried either?"

"We grow coffee and cocoa beans in the orc kingdom," he said. "Tea for leaves as well." Sucking in a deep breath, he released it. "I'll start with coffee."

"Coming right up." I placed a cup and saucer in front of him, noting his ill-fitting clothing, a basketball shirt with the number one on the front and too-snug jeans—though he might like them that way. Some guys did.

Manufacturers were scrambling to produce clothing that would fit orcs. Other than what they brought with them from their city, they'd been buying clothing made for super-tall bodybuilders.

After pouring piping hot coffee into his cup, I nudged my head to the small containers nearby. "Cream and sugar are there."

"Thank you." He flashed me a tusk-filled grin that made hummingbirds fly through my belly.

He was cute. Devastatingly so.

I hadn't dated an orc yet, but I was open to the idea. There was something appealing about them I couldn't define.

"I'm Deegar," he said with a nod.

"Cat. Short for Catherine."

"A pretty name."

My grin joined his. "Cat or Catherine?"

"Both." He sipped his coffee and studied my face.

"Order's up," my cook, Wilfred, called out, placing the mounded oversized plate on the shelf between the kitchen and the bar section of the diner.

"Let me know when you're ready to order." I turned and grabbed the dish to bring to a customer.

After serving the food, I strode back behind the island and up to Deegar. "What would you like?"

He scanned the menu again, his fingertip falling on the cheapest thing in the place.

Down on his luck?

There was no reason I couldn't make him feel welcome in our sweet little town. "If you're feeling adventurous, I can offer a full breakfast for only ninety-nine cents."

"Hey, you didn't tell me about that special," Joe griped, glaring at his almost-empty plate. "How come he rates?"

"Because he's cute." I flashed Deegar another grin. Truly, it felt good to smile. I'd wallowed in sadness since Mom died.

His golden eyes lit up, and my suspicion was confirmed when I spied relief in his gaze. "Seriously?"

I leaned across the counter and lowered my voice as if I was sharing a big secret. "It's just my way of giving back. Consider it a special deal for a new guy in town."

"You're right. I arrived not long ago. I'm here . . ." He cleared his throat, and his gaze dropped to his coffee. "I'm new."

We all knew what it was like to hit rock bottom. Maybe in addition to being new to the area, he didn't have a place to stay.

"The special includes two eggs any way you like them, bacon, hash browns, and either toast or pancakes. Everything's made fresh to order."

"I haven't tried pancakes," he said.

"We use my mom's special recipe." Made with a dash of vanilla.

"Sounds good. Eggs scrambled, then."

I noted four eggs on his order. He was a big, muscular guy.

His gaze scanned the small diner with glass walls making up the front. In the distance, the ocean sparkled. A few customers sat on the tiny deck beneath umbrellas, savoring the view. "You've got an amazing location here."

"Thanks. The diner belonged to my mom, though I worked here with her from the time I was sixteen." My smile faded. "She died a year ago of an aneurysm. It happened fast." Too fast. There'd been no time to say goodbye.

"I'm sorry."

"Thanks." My throat tight, I turned to place his order and continue serving my customers. The diner was open for breakfast and lunch Saturday through Wednesday, and I was the only server. When it was me, Mom, and Wilfred, we got by, but lately, I'd begun to think I needed to hire someone. I could only do two jobs for so long.

Wilfred completed Deegar's order, and I set it in front of him.

He gazed at it with appreciation. "It smells wonderful."

"Rumbling belly?" I nudged the syrup and bowl of butter packets his way.

"I'm famished. I feel like I haven't eaten in weeks."

So he *was* having a hard time.

While he dug in, I refilled his coffee. I rang up Marge and Dr. Yang, giving them both kisses on the cheek. Even Joe, who was still grumbling, got a hug. All of them were like parents to me now, and I couldn't imagine how I would've gotten by over the past year without their friendship.

The diner slowly cleared out until it was just me, Wilfred cleaning the grill, and Deegar. I bustled around, rolling silverware in cloth napkins and refilling the mustard and ketchup, prepping for the lunch crowd.

As I washed the menus, Deegar pushed his empty plate aside. "That was fantastic. I can't remember when I've eaten so well."

He reached into his pocket—

I shook my head and leaned close to him again. There was no one else who would hear, but I liked being near him. He smelled good, like a spice you would dab behind your ears. Or roll in. "Your breakfast today is on me. Consider it a gift from a friend."

"That's sweet of you. Thanks. I . . . I need to remember to carry cash."

"Many use cards. Have you set that up yet?"

All the orcs emerged from the mountain with bags of gold and jewels, making them incredibly wealthy—once they'd found the right buyers for their earthly treasure.

Deegar said he was new. He may not have had a chance to trade his in for cash.

"I haven't. I got here and well," He frowned, "I guess you could say I ran away."

I tilted my head. "From what?"

"Too many obligations."

"You don't come across as a guy who'd shirk something like that."

"Sometimes, it can be incredibly overwhelming. I needed a break."

"Breaks are good. To be honest, there have been times when I've felt like running away myself."

"Something we have in common."

My smile rose again, and his joined in. Damn, was he gorgeous with his dark hair brushing his big, burly shoulders, his majestic horns, and his jaw that looked chiseled by diamonds.

I took a deep breath and blurted out, "Do you need a place to stay?"

Surprise danced across his features. "What are you suggesting?"

My mind shot to all sorts of steamy ideas—none of them appropriate for conversation with a guy I'd just met. "The house I inherited from my mother is small, just one bedroom, but I've got a free couch if you need a place to stay until you get settled."

"I couldn't impose."

I shrugged. "I'm offering. It's no imposition."

After a brief pause, he nodded. "Thank you, Cat. This means a lot to me."

CHAPTER 2

DEEGAR

I was stunned by Cat's offer.

She stood on the other side of the bar wearing a confident smile, her dark blue eyes studying me.

I almost blurted out the truth. I didn't need her help. I had more money than I could spend in three lifetimes. Although I couldn't access it at this time, not without revealing my location.

Something about her intrigued me. She was pretty as far as humans went, extra curvy, the way I like females. Her eyes had caught my attention right away. Orcs only had varying shades of gold. Seeing green, blue, and even brown surprised me when I first arrived in the human world.

The air between us crackled. The low lights overhead cast a warm glow on her face, highlighting strands of pink in her long, dark hair. My orc senses tingled with interest. I'd like to get to know her better, and it was refreshing that she didn't realize who I was.

"That's generous of you," I said.

She shrugged. "No problem." She glanced at the clock hanging above the center of the bar. "The lunch crowd will begin arriving soon. If you want to come back here around three, I'll be done closing, and I'll take you to my house. We can walk there from here."

I stood. Her gaze scanned my frame, and I wondered what she thought of me. Some humans found orcs attractive. Others . . . well, we didn't need to mate with them all to maintain our species.

"I'll be back at three, then. Unless," I frowned, "would you like help? You appear short-staffed."

"Until Mom died, there were three of us. Wilfred cooks, and Mom and I waitressed. We're not open 24/7, just for breakfast and lunch, thankfully, but it's a lot for one person to handle."

"I could pitch in if you'd like."

"Do you have server experience?"

Not a bit. "I can figure it out." My grin came easy. I felt like doing it all the time while near Cat. "You fed me. You're offering me your couch. It's the least I can do to pay you back."

"It's an old couch, though it's still comfy."

"I appreciate your willingness to help me."

"You seem to need a boost, and I've got one available."

"So do I."

I could see her wavering. She came across as someone who didn't like to ask for help even if she was in need. It made me admire her. She was refreshing, exciting. "We'll have to fill out some paperwork. I guess we have time."

"I'd be happy to do so." I wasn't sure how long I could remain hidden in this little coastal Maine town, but I'd aim for a week before I let anyone know where I was.

It was past time for Deegar to escape the confines of his tight world and live.

"I appreciate it." She nudged her chin toward the back, where we sat and filled out forms.

Wilfred had already left for a break.

"Time to load and run the dishwasher," she said after we'd finished the paperwork. We stacked all the dirty dishes inside and started the device.

Next, I helped her top off the salt and pepper shakers and sanitize all the tables, booths, chairs, and door handles.

Not long after we finished emptying the dishwasher, customers started to arrive. Soon, the diner was full of people waiting outside to be seated.

"Just tell me what to do," I said as Wilfred got the grill going.

She handed me a pad of paper and a pen. "Take one table at a time. I'll handle the rest. I'm glad you're eager to work, but I don't want to overwhelm you."

"I appreciate that."

"No worries." She patted my arm. "We all start somewhere."

The diner remained busy until after two. Serving tables was tough work. Customers were picky, and some were impatient. Didn't they realize food was better when the cook had time to prepare it carefully? That was something I'd found common in humans—a need to rush around as if whatever they had to do next would disappear if they didn't get to it in time.

After the last guest left and Cat locked the door, turning the sign to closed, she leaned against the back and blew her breath upward. Her dark bangs shot through with pink lifted before dropping back down onto her forehead. "Done. You did a great job for your first time. The customers love you."

"Damn straight," Wilfred called out from the kitchen. "Awesome to have you here, Deegar."

"Thank you." I scratched the back of my neck and looked back and forth between them. "You think I did alright?"

"You didn't see how Bernice gushed or how her husband scowled?" Cat said.

"You didn't drop a dish, and that's a win in my book," Wilfred said with humor shining in his voice. The older man came over to stand in the opening between the kitchen and the main section of the diner. "I'm out of here. I got the dishwasher going again."

"Thanks." Cat gave him a quick hug.

"Always welcome, little one," he said gruffly. With a wave to me, he left through the back.

"Some people find his scowl intimidating," she said lightly, watching me.

"He's a great guy." Anyone who helped Cat had my full regard.

"We can head to my place now. Do you have a bag?" She peered around me as if she expected luggage to materialize.

"I don't."

"We'll take care of that also." She strode into the kitchen. "This way. We'll use the back exit. I'll see if Mom left any of Dad's old clothing. He was a big guy, though not as tall as you. You could wear those until we pick up a few things."

I winced. "You don't need to buy me clothing." Why hadn't I thought to grab a few outfits—and cash—before I fled?

Because I was tired of the life I'd led, and I'd needed a clean break. And I wasn't used to doing much for myself.

Damn, was I soft.

"When I pay you, you can buy your own things, but payday is on Thursday and it's only Tuesday. I'll float you some cash. I know a great thrift place, though they're closed today. We'll go tomorrow."

I owed her so much already, for being kind and generous, and for giving me employment.

Maybe I hadn't thought this through enough. I saw my chance to leave and did, not knowing where I'd end up. I boarded a bus, spending all the cash I had for my ticket, and got off at the last stop—here.

We left the empty diner, stepping out into the late afternoon sunshine. Fall had arrived with trees changing colors and a crispness in the air that hinted at winter.

"What's it like in the orc kingdom?" she asked as we walked down a street. A few humans gawked at me while others ignored us. We didn't encounter other orcs, but I assumed some must live in town.

Hopefully they wouldn't recognize me.

I pondered her question for a moment, trying to find the right words. I decided to give her some truth without revealing my identity yet. "As you know, it's hidden deep within a long mountain range. We have big cities in enormous underground valleys. We live a lot like humans, strangely enough."

"What did you do while you lived there?"

"I was . . . part of the administration."

"I see." She urged me to turn right at an intersection, taking a street leading away from the sea. "I read a new delegation had arrived to add to the treaty. Are you with them?" Her rueful laugh rang out. "Wait. Of course you're not. If you were, you wouldn't be here in Settler's Cove. You'd be with the others, sitting in a conference room and not," she spread her arms and spun around laughing, "not enjoying the smell of the sea and everything this cute little town has to offer."

"You like it here."

"I love it." Her eyes gleamed. "I was born a few towns

over, and I've lived here since I could crawl. After my dad died when I was eight, Mom sold the bigger house they'd lived in and bought a cottage. She left it and the diner to me."

"A job and a home."

"Right? It's more than most have." Her face fell. "I'm sorry. I don't mean to make you feel bad about your situation."

I tried not to cringe. It felt wrong to be dishonest with her, but it was freeing not to have an entourage with me wherever I went. Even more, it was freeing to talk with a woman without her gushing about my role in the kingdom. "I do well, and, hey, I worked today and my paycheck's coming."

"You made tips, too."

"Yes, it felt strange to have people give me money."

"Servers don't make much. Mom paid me well, and I kept my tips, so you'll see the same." Her cheeks pinkened. "I mean, if you want to work with me another day."

Before I could shout yes, she turned toward a small cottage painted light blue with white trim. A white picket fence with chipped paint surrounded the patch of grass in front. It was pretty, with flowers blooming in boxes beneath the windows as well as along the stone path marching toward the front door nestled in the middle of a front porch.

She creaked the gate open, and we stepped inside.

After closing it, she led me up to her house, unlocking the front door and urging me inside.

"Welcome to my humble abode," she said with a happy smile. "It was sad to be here right after Mom died but now the memory of her working at the kitchen counter or sitting on the porch makes me smile. I'm trying to focus on the good because life's too short to wallow in the bad. Having her in my life for twenty-eight years was a gift I'm grateful to have."

"I've painted," I said.

"Oh, really?" She shut the door behind us and turned toward the open living area with a couch, a TV, a recliner chair, and long wall shelf overloaded with books. "Do you paint landscapes or . . ."

"I could paint your fence to thank you for your generosity."

"That's sweet of you." She huffed. "It's one more in a long list of tasks I need to do. The diner keeps me busy five days a week, and frankly, when I'm off, I like to putter in the garden or walk on the beach."

"I've dabbled in various mediums, experimenting to find my true passion." With my father running everything, I had to keep busy. Music and art were encouraged. "Who knows? Maybe someday I'll create something that moves people. Anyway, I'll paint your fence, freeing you to do the things you enjoy."

"It sounds like you plan to be in town for a while."

Her voice came out neutral, but I realized I was making assumptions. "I meant if I stayed here long."

"That's up to you. My couch is yours for as long as you need it."

Fortunately, it was an oversized couch. At least my feet wouldn't hang off the end.

"The house has a kitchen-dining room combo on the left." She gestured. "And truly only one bedroom. The room I slept in before I moved into an apartment is tiny, and Mom made it into an office after I was gone. When I moved back in, I put all my boxes there." She placed her purse on the kitchen counter and turned, leaning against it. "I want so much."

"What do you mean?"

"The diner has done well. I'd love to open another a few towns over."

"Then do it."

"It takes money, and I'm tapped out at the moment. Hospitals don't provide care for free, and when she died, I had to pay the lawyers to settle her estate. But I'll get ahead again and then watch out world because I'm coming! Like you, I want to create something that moves people, only on a smaller scale. I'll settle for yummy meals in people's bellies."

"It's a worthy goal." What would she say if I offered her enough money to fulfill her dream?

I suspected it would change things between us.

"I believe in you, Cat," I said. "And if there's anything I can do to help, count me in."

She smiled, and her blue eyes shone like the stars I'd admired the first time I arrived in the human world. "I will, Deegar. Thanks." She looked over at me with a mischievous glint in her eye. "Now that I've shared my hopes and dreams, tell me what you want out of life."

I pondered her question for a moment. It was rare for someone to ask me about my own desires separate from the expectations that came with my role in the kingdom, one that was mapped out before the day I was born.

"I want to be completely happy," I said softly. "To find something that fulfills me, regardless of what others think."

"Any ideas how to bring that about?"

"I've started already." Running was the first step.

A smile tugged at the corners of her lips. "Stick with me, and you'll discover a whole new world, starting with my secret muffin recipe and my skill with thrift store finds." She nudged her head toward the fridge. "It's four thirty. Are you hungry? I could whip something up."

"Why don't I help?"

We made a simple meal of long white strings boiled in water Cat told me were made of eggs and flour, and we topped the strands with a red sauce crafted from ground meat, more tomatoes than I'd seen in one place, and spices.

"This tastes amazing," I said, scooping up another full bite and shoving it into my mouth as we sat on stools at the kitchen counter.

"They say a way to a man's heart is through his stomach," she said with a laugh.

They might be right. I liked Cat a lot already.

"We made plenty of pasta, so dish up a second plate if you'd like."

After washing the dishes, another new thing for me, we went into the living room and sat on the couch. She was right; it was very comfortable. She lifted a long black box and pointed it toward the TV. I'd only seen televisions playing as I passed through rooms, and they intrigued me. So many moving pictures and sounds.

"What would you like to watch?" she asked.

I shrugged. "Honestly, I've never watched TV."

Her eyes widened. "Never?"

"Never."

"I'll introduce you to the land of make believe." She frowned as she flicked through screens listing options.

It was almost overwhelming. "How does one choose?"

"Whatever appeals. What are your thoughts about a romcom?" Her lips twitched and her eyes sparkled as she awaited my answer.

"I don't know what they are."

She gasped, but I could tell it was a tease. "You're a romcom virgin."

"You've discovered my secret."

Her sunny smile made mine lift as well. "I'll introduce you to romcoms with my favorite one, Mate For A Minute."

As the movie played, I stole glances at Cat, paying more attention to her than the show. Her enthusiasm for the film was infectious, and her laughter filled the room.

While I tried to focus on the story and punchlines, my senses were entirely preoccupied with studying the way her lips formed a smile and how her laughter trilled out, making her face glow.

She was infinitely appealing, and I already couldn't imagine not having her in my life.

Finally, the movie ended, and she shut off the TV, sighing with joy. "I love a happy ever after, don't you?"

I never thought there'd be one in my future, but being with Cat suggested it might be possible.

"Tell me about your childhood," Cat said, settling deeper into the couch cushions, facing me. She tucked her leg beneath her body. "Are you an only child like me, or do you have siblings?"

"Like you, I'm the only one." There was no one to share the burden of my looming responsibilities. Except . . . "My cousin grew up with me, however. She's a few years younger."

"What was it like growing up in the orc kingdom?"

Long days of studies to prepare me for my future role. Working with various weapons until I'd mastered them all. Training late into the night sometimes, too. "The kingdom is amazing."

"Maybe someday, I'll visit."

"I bet you'd enjoy it." I imagined what I could show her. "The Caves of Shafaar. The falls between the main city's valley and the next. We could swim in the light lavender pools and climb all the way to the top of the distant mountains to touch the snow." All things I'd wanted to do but was told they'd interfere with my duties. My time was never my own. "In many ways, I grew up in a world where everything seems perfect—no real struggles or true hardships."

Cat tilted her head. "It sounds like a fairytale."

"It is." For me, anyway. "But with all that perfection comes responsibility." I held the future of the kingdom in my hands.

"Kind of like the way I grew up. I started working at the diner at sixteen, and I stayed on after I finished school. Mom needed the help, you know? And I wanted to be here for her. I'm grateful I didn't move to the city. If I had, I would've missed out on these past years working beside her. We were like sisters. She had my same long brown hair, and her smile could warm even the coldest heart." Her lips trembled. "I miss her a lot."

I tugged her into my side and put my arm around her. "I'm sorry."

She leaned into me. "Life's amazing, but sometimes, it sucks."

"It sure does."

Her laugh snorted out. "Thank you for hanging out with me. I'm lonely here."

"I've enjoyed being with you. I get lonely too."

"In your fairytale orc kingdom? How's that possible?"

"Because duty awaits me each morning, and it keeps me in its clutches long after I've retired at the end of the day."

Cat's eyes softened as she looked up at me. "It takes

courage to step out of your comfort zone, to seek something more. Look at you, leaving the fairytale behind and moving to the human world. I admire you. That's courageous."

Her words made my heart flip over. "I'm just an orc trying to find his place in this complex human world."

"Don't undermine yourself, Deegar. I can already tell there's more to you than meets the eye."

I held my breath. "What could I be hiding?"

"That's just it. I feel like you are, but you can't be. You're open. I can see that already. I like it."

Despite our different backgrounds, there was an undeniable connection between us—a shared understanding of what it meant to have dreams and aspirations.

We sat in silence, welcome after the bustle of the day. I liked lounging on her couch with her warmth by my side. Our feet were propped on her low table, something that would never be permitted back home.

When her yawns started multiplying, I sadly released her.

"I guess I should get to bed," she said, rising. "You must be tired too. I've got some extra things in my bathroom you can use. Oh! I mentioned seeing if Dad has anything that might fit you."

She hurried from the room, taking stairs down to another level, returning within a few moments. "Mom must've gotten rid of them. The boxes are gone. I'm sorry. I don't believe anything of mine will fit."

"I agree." The top of her head only came to my mid-chest.

I looked down at the silly outfit I'd traded for the elaborate costume I wore when I fled. "I can wear this." Frankly, this entire situation was humbling. I was used to telling my butler what I wanted to wear, and he'd make it appear. Now the only clothing I possessed was what I wore on my back.

Cat didn't seem to mind that I had nothing.

"You'll want to change eventually," she said. "And shower in the morning."

"I have an undergarment on. Will it do for sleep?"

Her face cleared. "I suppose you can wear that. Toss your clothing into the hall." She nudged her head in that direction. "I'll run them through the washer and the dryer when I get up in the morning. At least they'll be clean for you to wear tomorrow. We can go to the thrift store after work."

Standing, I stripped off the shirt and nudged the pants down around my ankles.

"Wait, wait," she said weakly. She gulped as her gaze slid down my frame like a caress. "Do you, um, work out a lot?"

I peered down at my body. "I practice various battle techniques."

"With what kind of weapon?"

"A long sword. Mace. Everything, actually. I need to be well versed in them all."

"Why?" She couldn't seem to direct her attention to

my face, and truly, I didn't mind. My cock liked her stare and started shifting behind the thin cotton of my undergarment.

"In case I need to use one of them to defend myself."

"Who'd bother to attack you?"

Everyone. There were many who'd be happy to eliminate me if they thought they could elevate themselves or one of their select family members to my place in line for the throne. "It's good to know how to defend myself."

"I guess you could be robbed." She shook her head and held out her hand for the clothing.

"Yes, that's it."

"I'll get the washer going. Goodnight." Without another word, she spun and ran from the room.

CHAPTER 3
CAT

"Order's up," Wilfred called out, dropping a full plate onto the sill between the kitchen and bar.

Deegar was escorting Marge and her best friend, Harriet, to a booth. Harriet walked a few steps behind them, her head tilted to gape at Deegar's ass. I couldn't blame her. It was cute and slightly rounded. He gestured for them to sit at the booth and handed them menus.

Marge introduced him to Harriet, and her cheeks brightened. She patted her purple-hued gray hair she had styled twice a week and grinned, revealing her pearly dentures.

He took her hand and bowed over it.

"Go on, now," Harriet said, tugging her hand away. "You'd think I was a princess or something."

"All women are princesses," he declared.

With a grin, I grabbed the order and hurried it over to

Dr. Yang. "Here you go. Let me top off your coffee." He'd drained the cup.

He craned his neck to look around. "I thought Deegar was my server today." This morning, Deegar had taken more than one booth.

"He's busy with Marge and Harriet."

Dr. Yang huffed but smiled my way. "He's got a certain way about him, doesn't he? He's quite the orc prince charming."

"That, he is." I loved how he interacted with the customers. His playful banter and quick wit had everyone eating out of his muscular hands. Even the regulars, who usually stuck to their same seat at the counter, were eager to be seated in Deegar's section.

He moved gracefully when he strode through a room, almost like a dancer—or someone who was highly skilled in battle, as he'd admitted. Why the need to train so much other than for interest? I'd read the orcs hadn't warred in many generations. We'd asked during the initial treaty negotiations. If they planned to bring their battles to the surface, our governments would've laid down some heavy ground rules.

I found myself stealing glances at him whenever I could, enjoying everything about him. The way his eyes crinkled at the corners when he smiled, or how his voice rumbled like thunder when he laughed—all of it made my heart do somersaults in my chest.

If I didn't know better, I'd think I was falling for him.

But no, I couldn't let myself do something like that.

He was a friend, someone to help and make my evenings a little less lonely.

After the breakfast crowd left and before we prepped for lunch, he and I sat on the tiny back deck in the shade eating grilled cheese sandwiches, washing it down with iced tea.

"Excellent meal," he said, sitting back and patting his belly.

"You're sure I can't make you another?" He'd consumed four sandwiches and was on his third glass of tea.

Wilfred had taken a break and would be back in an hour.

"I could probably eat more." He grinned my way. "But I'm full enough for now."

I'd have to think up something amazing for dinner. I didn't often cook for myself since Mom died. Having someone around to appreciate my efforts was fun.

"You've got . . ." Frowning, he leaned his face close to mine and brushed crumbs off my chin.

"Thanks."

He kept his head near mine while he studied my face. "You're very pretty, Cat. Have I told you that yet?"

"Um, I don't think so." My cheeks heated. "Thanks again."

"I want to kiss you. Would you ever consider kissing an orc?"

Only one—him. "Are you asking for permission?"

His face scrunched. "I never have, but I don't want to ruin this."

"I'm not sure asking before kissing someone could be considered a mistake." What would his tusks feel like against my lips? My breathing growing tight. I wanted to find out.

"I'll take that as a yes." He cupped my face gently, something I wouldn't think possible for a big guy like him. His mouth claimed mine, and his tusks were surprisingly soft, brushing my lips. His hands held me firmly but tenderly, as if he was afraid of breaking me.

The kiss deepened as our tongues touched, sending a jolt of electricity through me that made me gasp in pleasure. His taste was sweet, and I found myself wanting more of him with every passing second.

The kiss ended too soon, leaving me breathless and dazed by the intensity of it. We opened our eyes, and I stared at him in amazement that appeared to be mirrored in his golden gaze.

"That was nice," I said softly.

He grinned, his tusks jutting up from his lower jawline in a way that made him even more attractive than before our kiss. "I think it was more than nice."

"It was short."

"Are you complaining?" His hands slid to my shoulders, holding me in place. "I'd be more than happy to keep kissing you until it's time to get back to work."

"No complaints." My core throbbed from a simple kiss, and I wasn't sure what to make of that.

Was I ready to start a relationship with someone new?

Something banged in the kitchen, telling me Wilfred had returned. The last thing I wanted was for him to find me making out on the back deck with my new server. There was nothing wrong with me dating Deegar, assuming one kiss and a shared meal—plus him sleeping on my sofa—could be considered dating. But was I ready to announce to the world that I liked him?

I'd think about it during the next shift.

"Back to work," I said in a voice much too breathless. You'd think I'd run around the block or something.

"Yes, work." We rose, and he frowned down at me with an intensity that made my body grow hotter.

"What?" I asked, fanning my face.

"I . . ." He shook his head and gave me a smile. "Nothing."

CHAPTER 4
DEEGAR

Cat was my true mate, and I wasn't sure what to do about it.

If I was back in the orc kingdom, she would've known this when we kissed like I did.

Then I'd fling her over my shoulder and bolt into the woods. She'd *encourage* me to do this. Orc males had nesting spots prepared for just such a moment. I'd take her there, and we'd complete the mate bond in bed, not emerging until our heat had waned.

How could I tell Cat I would soon be nearly ravenous to possess her body?

I'd have to mention something soon. Walking around with an erection wouldn't do.

We worked until the last customer left, then cleaned everything, getting it ready for the next shift, though we had two days off before that. Once everything was settled, we locked the front door and strolled in the opposite direction of where Cat lived.

"I thought we could pick up some chicken to bake for dinner. I can make broccoli and cauliflower with a cheese sauce, and if you're really sweet to me," she shot me a grin, "I'll make my secret roasted potato recipe."

"You're my true mate," I blurted out. Heat kept roaring through my veins, each time finding its way to my cock.

She stopped on the corner and despite the boxed walking figure on the pole indicating we could cross, she remained in place, frowning at me. "Excuse me?"

"I'm going into heat, and unless we have sex a billion times between now and when it wanes, I'll need to find a cave and suffer until it ends."

"I . . ." Her head tilted. "Is this some kind of joke?"

"No joke. Have you read about orc mating customs?"

She shrugged. "Only a little."

"When an orc finds their true mate, which for me is you, they go into heat."

"Like a hot flash?"

I didn't know what that was. "True mates are rare, but when an orc finds theirs, they take them to a secluded spot where they have lots of sex."

A woman pushing a carriage with a tiny infant inside stopped beside us. With a smirk, she waved to the child. "*This* is what can happen when you have lots of sex."

"Your infant is gorgeous," I said. Someday, I'd love to

have an orcling or two. It was very easy to see Cat holding our first.

"Thanks. She's a sweetie." After giving us a look I couldn't define, the other woman hurried across the street.

Cat's frown deepened. "Are you feeling okay?"

"When we kissed, I knew you were the one."

"We said it was a *nice* kiss. Not groundbreaking or . . . heat-inducing."

"It was an amazing kiss. Our first. I'll treasure the memory always."

"Explain more about matings and . . . heat, which I suspect has nothing to do with the temperature around us."

At least she wasn't running from me or backing away in horror. "When we find our true mate, we have certain rituals we follow."

"Like what?" We crossed the street.

"I don't have a nest, and I apologize for that."

"A nest?" Her eyebrows lifted, and she strode all the way around me, stopping in front of me. "I don't see wings. You're not a bird with a nest." Her lips twitched with humor, but her gaze was completely serious.

"Males have a nest waiting in case they meet their true mate."

"If it's rare, why not wait until—if—you meet her first?"

I shrugged. "This is how it's done."

"Did you have a nest prepared in the orc kingdom?"

"I did."

"Yet you didn't meet your true mate there."

"Because she's you."

Cat shook her head as if denying my statement. "Why the nest?"

"Because I'm supposed to do this." Lifting her, I flung her over my shoulder. I pivoted and raced back across the street, car horns blaring and people shouting.

"What . . .? What . . .?" Cat cried.

When we reached her home, I opened the door and went inside. I didn't stop until we'd reached her bedroom, where I laid her gently on the surface.

"Your bed will have to substitute for my nest," I declared, climbing up over her.

"I . . ." Her hands cupped my shoulders, and her voice deepened. "For whatever reason, I find this very appealing. Is it possible for a human to go into heat?"

"Among orcs, it's very common. I'm going to make love to you over and over, Cat, and I promise you won't want to end this. You'll be completely satisfied."

CHAPTER 5
CAT

While I was wildly intrigued by this true mate process and, frankly, turned on by his words, I didn't know him very well. Certainly not well enough to . . . mate with him.

"Shouldn't you ask me if I want days of wild sex?" I said. My body shouted, *yes, yes, please.*

I did my best to shut it down.

"If you were an orc female, you'd know immediately, like me. You'd welcome me taking you to my nest."

"We're in *my* nest, evidently."

"We could call it *ours.*"

"We don't know each other very well." Although that wasn't completely true. In my heart, I felt like we'd known each other forever, as if we were together in a past life. As if we'd sought each other.

"Unless you tell me no, I'm going to kiss you," he growled.

"Do it." I craved another taste.

A smile flashed across his mouth. Leaning forward, he captured my lips in the sweetest kiss. Hunger soon replaced the sweetness, and I grabbed onto his shoulders, tugging him down on top of me.

Maybe I *was* also going into heat, though I'd never heard of that happening with women. But I'd also never wanted anyone as much as I did Deegar.

Moaning, I bucked my hips up toward him, encountering something very large I'd tried not to notice last night when he stripped down to his snug boxers.

We broke apart, and he stared down at me with so much affection in his eyes, it pulled me in. "Can I show you what a true mate does for his beloved?"

If a human man said this, I'd know it was a line, but Deegar was taking this so seriously. He meant what he said, and it was refreshing.

"What exactly are you offering?" It wasn't a bad thing to be cautious.

"Let me touch you, taste you. That'll be enough to satisfy my heat for now."

I'd be foolish to fall into bed—*nest*—with a guy this fast, right? One hundred percent yes. Still, the words rushed from my mouth. "Show me."

With a grin, he lifted one finger and a claw snapped out of . . . somewhere on the tip. I'd check his hands out later. He carefully slipped it under my shirt and bra, and before I could gasp, he sliced through the material as if it was tissue paper. Parting the shreds, he kissed my neck, nibbling on my skin while my mind succumbed once more.

This was crazy. *We* were crazy.

He couldn't mean all this. But in my heart, I hoped he did.

Finding my mouth again, he drank from it, each of his kisses deeper than the last.

His hands moved lower, tracing my body. I was on fire as he kissed along my jawline and then lower to my breasts. My skin burned where his lips touched me, and sparks of electricity shot through me. His hands were strong and sure as they explored my curves, sending an uncontrollable shiver through my limbs.

He growled against my skin, a low rumble that sent a thrill through me. The sound made it clear that he wanted me, and the realization filled me with joy.

My heart thundered as his touch grew bolder and more insistent. Everywhere his hands roamed, I felt alive; everywhere his mouth tasted, I felt loved; everywhere he touched me, I felt desired beyond measure. He was showing me what it meant to be wanted—to be cherished—and it was beautiful beyond belief.

His hand was gentle yet possessive, making it clear that I belonged to him, and I wasn't sure what I thought of that. But as he sucked my nipple into his mouth and ran his tongue across it, I was beyond caring. Everything inside me was wrapped up in this moment.

The heat of his breath against my skin caused goosebumps to rise while his tusks gently grazed over my nipples, sending a shockwave of pleasure straight to my core.

I was melting into him as he moved lower, his tongue tracing circles around my navel. He kept going, first slicing through my jeans and underwear, then pushing it aside.

"You're beautiful, my lovely mate," he said reverently against my skin. "I want to taste you more than I've ever wanted anything in my life."

At my nod, he parted my thighs and kissed lower until he reached the apex between my legs.

He stroked down my saturated slit and sucked his fingers into his mouth, his gaze locked on mine. "You taste amazing, like sunshine and the sweetest berries."

That couldn't be true, but he sucked me deeper into this time with him. Nothing and no one could draw me away.

With a smile, he licked from my opening up to my clit. "So sweet. Perfect." While his hands massaged my sides and hips, he circled my clit with his tongue before tugging it into his mouth.

Like I was a rocket, I burst upward, moaning.

He lingered on my clit for what felt like an eternity; exploring every bit of it with an expertise I'd never experienced before. The sensation of him loving me in this way was nearly overwhelming. I gasped and pumped my hips up to him, clutching his horns. When I stroked them, he growled against my flesh.

He slipped a finger into my passage and growled

again. "Wet," he barked before diving back onto my clit. Another finger joined the first, and he pumped them, gliding them across my inner walls while I cried out with pleasure.

I writhed beneath him, my body trembling as he increased the pressure and intensity of his movements. His tongue flicked against my clit as his fingers continued their exploration. I could feel my orgasm building, radiating from my core and spreading outwards until I was about to be consumed by it.

My breathing was ragged, and my heart raced as he began to slide his fingers in and out of me faster and faster. With each thrust, a wave of pleasure ripple through my body. It intensified when he added a third finger to the mix. The sensation was almost too much for me to bear; it felt like all the energy in my body had been focused on this one moment, this one feeling that was so intense it almost hurt.

He continued flicking his tongue across my clit while thrusting into me with an expert rhythm that brought me closer and closer to the edge.

I tipped over into oblivion, crying out as I came undone in his arms. He held onto me as I rode out the waves until they subsided, and I lay gasping for breath.

He slowly drew his fingers out of me and licked them carefully. "You're amazing, mate. Simply amazing."

CHAPTER 6
DEEGAR

She was my true mate, and my heat was upon me.

While I'd like to remain in my improvised nest with her until my heat waned, it wouldn't be fair. She enjoyed the life she had in this town, and it would be wrong of me to do anything to interfere with that.

"I'm not sure what to think of all this . . . mating stuff," she said as we left her house and continued with our errand.

"I imagine it's not easy to adjust to. I've learned enough about human culture to know that you don't have true mates and humans don't go into heat."

"You said you want sex."

"All the time, but what we've done so far has satisfied me for now."

"I like you, Deegar. I . . ." Frowning, she shook her head. "I like you *a lot*. But it sounds like you're suggesting we spend a lifetime together."

"That's the way it is with true mates. We meet, have lots of sex." I grinned when she ruefully shook her head. "And we remain together forever. True mates fall in love quickly."

"I've never been in love," she said wistfully. We turned right at a corner, walking down the next sidewalk. "But surely you can't be falling in love with me already."

I sensed I'd frighten her if I told her I was. "It's easier for the male."

"Why?" We entered a grocery store and walked down the aisles.

"I guess I should say it's easier for an orc male. From the time we're little, we're told about true mates and how we must ask the fates to send us ours. We're told that we'll know when we kiss, and we're instructed on how to build our nests."

"You said it's rare. Maybe you're mistaken?" She picked out chicken, placed it in her basket, and strode up the next aisle.

Walking with her, I pressed my fist against my chest. "I know it's true here. But you can have a day or two to come to the same conclusion."

Her laughter snorted out, but she quickly sobered. "You're not joking."

I shook my head. "I'd never tease about something like this."

"What if I tell you no?" she asked softly, selecting vegetables, adding them with the chicken.

"Then I'll return to the orc kingdom and go to one of the caves. They're set up for males to remain in until their heat wanes. And after that, I'll stay as far away from you as I can. I wouldn't want to trigger my heat again. It can be . . . quite painful."

"You said I have a few days to think about this?"

"Yes." A mating could never be forced.

"Alright." She remained pensive as we paid and left the store, walking to another. I opened the door for her, and we went inside.

"We need a cell phone," she told the clerk, who took us to a display of devices.

I was offered a phone when I first arrived in the human realm, but I turned it down. Once the treaty was signed, I wasn't going to remain here, and the phone wouldn't work in the orc kingdom.

Now all I could focus on was making sure I got Cat's number.

It didn't take long to add my phone to her plan, and we left with my new device in my pocket—and her number programmed in.

"Next is the thrift store," she said, taking my hand.

I linked our fingers, enjoying being close to her this way.

"You'll take the cost of the phone out of my wages," I insisted.

"We'll see." She shot me a shy smile. "They gave you an incredible deal, and it doesn't cost much to add another line to my plan."

We entered the thrift store and strolled through the aisles.

"They only have a few items that'll fit an orc," she said with a twist of her lips. "You'd think now that orcs live here, they'd have more. I'm sorry. I thought we could completely outfit you with one stop." She held up a tunic made of a stretchy material with a swooping symbol. "This might fit." She pressed it against my upper body, frowning. "The color's okay, don't you think?"

"It has another male's name on the front." I wasn't complaining, not when the selection was this limited.

"Nike's a brand, not a person's name."

I stared down at the black shirt with pink writing. "Alright."

She nodded and laid the shirt over her arm. "Here's another." This one was blue with yellow writing, still with the other name. "Sweatpants might work well, though we'll look for jeans in your size. What *is* your size?"

"I don't know."

"I'm sure it's hard to compare our sizes to yours. What size are you in . . . orc clothing?"

"I don't know that either." I peered around. "Is there a clerk who could help us?"

"Not here. But we can look in the big and tall section; maybe we'll find something there." She led me to another aisle where she sorted through the clothing.

So many items and almost none that would fit me.

"Okay, what about these?" she held blue pants

against my frame. "They're capris on you." Shaking her head, she returned them to the rack and pulled out another garment. "I think we're going to have to go with these." The gray pants had a drawstring at the waist and were cuffed at the ankle. And they were long enough not to be considered *cap-rees*.

"Why don't you try them on?" She led me to the back of the room and urged me behind a curtain where she hung the garments on a hook and stepped out, closing the cloth behind her. "You can change in here. Come on out when you're wearing them."

I removed my clothing and pulled on the gray pants. They were snug, but perhaps that was the fashion. I added the black tunic with what I still suspected as another male's name emblazoned on the front and stepped beyond the curtain where Cat was waiting.

Her lips trembled, and her eyes sparkled. "These aren't going to work."

I looked down at where the pants outlined my thighs and cock. "Why not?"

"Change. We'll keep looking." Pivoting, she stalked over to a chair and sat, leaning forward to cup her chin in her palms.

I returned to the tiny space and removed the items, donning my original clothing.

We purchased the shirts and left, walking down the street to another store where we bought items Cat called athleticwear. Everything had numbers and other people's names, and I wasn't sure why.

Returning to her home, we cooked the chicken, and I helped her make the cheese sauce. It was amazing. I could eat a vat of it plain.

I consumed more than I should have, but it all tasted wonderful. After, we sat on the sofa where she explained how to use the cell phone.

"I don't know anyone but you," I pointed out, unsure I truly needed this device.

"You'll make other friends, and you'll want to call them."

I nodded slowly.

"We could set up your social media presence if you'd like." She showed me how to take a shelfi—no, a *selfie*—and then I took a bunch of photos of us playing around and laughing on her sofa. Those, I'd treasure always.

What would I do if she decided she didn't want to be my mate?

CHAPTER 7
CAT

"I'm not sure what a social media presence is." His lips quirked up on one side. Incredibly cute.

"We can start with an email account and maybe . . . Chatbook?"

"Sure."

I hooked him up with an email account, then we created a Chatbook page. Within minutes, he had a direct message. That . . . was weird.

"What's that?" he asked, pointing at the screen.

I explained and urged him to open the message.

I've created a fan group for you, Deegar, a cute-faced woman gushed. *No worries about how to handle it. I'll do all the work!* She ended with three smiley emojis and seven faces throwing a kiss emojis. And her phone number.

"What does this mean?" he asked, his head tilting.

I explained, and color flooded his face.

"How can I tell her no?" he asked, frowning at the screen.

"Just say so."

He typed a reply.

Hers popped up almost immediately. *Please? You're so gorgeous. I promise it won't be any work for you. I'll do it all!!* She added five smiley emojis and ten kisses.

Jeez. My stomach shouldn't burn with irritation. She was an unknown woman on the internet, not sitting in the living room with Deegar like me.

He looked at me as if I should have a say in this decision.

I shrugged and swallowed back the lump in my throat. He was gorgeous. I could see why women would get excited about him.

"What exactly would a fan group do?" he asked.

"I guess show off your picture and talk about you."

"They don't know anything about me."

They wouldn't need to. What they didn't know, they'd make up.

"It would be a private group. Only those invited or who ask to join the group would have access to what's posted there."

His gaze slid away from mine. "I don't want my image or any information about me discussed by others, though I'm well aware I have little control over it."

I nodded, understanding his concern. I couldn't imagine anyone starting a fan club dedicated to me.

"That's the thing about being in the public eye. People will always talk, whether you want them to or not."

He sighed, running a hand through his thick, dark hair. "It's just . . . I've always valued my privacy, Cat. I don't know if I can handle having this kind of attention from strangers."

"I get it, Deegar. It's your decision, and whatever you choose, I'll support you."

He looked relieved, a faint smile tugging at his lips. "Thank you. That means a lot to me." He sent another message, and it was all I could do not to read over his shoulder. "I told her I don't want any part of this." His phone lit up with another direct message. "She says she'll keep it private." He sucked in a breath and released it. "Can I forbid this?"

"Unfortunately, no." I shook my head. "I'm sorry your first social media experience was disconcerting."

"I don't quite see the point of social media."

"It's a good place to connect with friends. With life rushing past us so fast, it's easy to miss things. I've learned of old family friends' deaths on Chatbook. Or seen when someone got a new pet. Information's posted quickly, and it can be fun to scroll through. But you need to be careful. People will post stuff that's not true."

"They'd lie?"

"Easily if it suited their agenda."

"Sounds like life in the orc kingdom only without a phone or social media. The only difference is it might take longer for you to hear the rumors or lies."

"It sounds like you've had some bad experiences."

"Unfortunately, yes."

We sat in a silence for a moment before he spoke again. "Would you join the fan group?"

I blinked, caught off guard by his question. "Me? Why would I join a fan group for you?"

His eyes sparkled mischievously. "Because you're my biggest fan."

A playful smirk made its way onto my face as I wagged a finger at him. "Oh really? Is that so?"

He leaned closer, his breath warm against my cheek. "You must be, because I'm yours."

"I'm afraid no one's made a fan club for me."

"They're missing out on someone special, then. I'd be the first member of your group."

"Maybe I *should* join your group. I could see what they're saying."

"And report to me?"

"If you'd like."

"Would you?"

"You could join yourself. If she ends up with more than one member—two if you count me—they might want to chat *with* you."

"There's only one woman I'm interested in chatting with, Cat. You."

The way he said my name so tenderly made my heart flip over. I felt like everything I'd gone through over the past year since Mom died had led me to this moment and him. I was falling in love with him.

"I'll join and let you know if they say anything you might like to know," I said. Rising, I looked his way. He was comically taller than me, so much so that we were at eye level with me standing. "I think it's probably time for me to go to bed."

He nodded. "Right. I'll be on the sofa again."

I hesitated for a moment. Was it too soon? Everything inside me said no, but there was one thread of self-preservation that told me I barely knew him, that I needed more time before I gave him my heart, body, and soul.

"Goodnight," I said softly at my door, still feeling uncertain.

"Goodnight, mate. Sleep well."

CHAPTER 8
DEEGAR

The diner was closed the next day. After breakfast, we sat on her tiny front porch, drinking coffee and sucking in the amazing scent of the sea.

"There are lakes and rivers in the orc kingdom," I said, savoring the beverage and Cat's company. The sun was warm on my lower legs where I'd tugged up my gray pants, and it dappled the sidewalk dusted with orange, red, and gold leaves.

I could tell already it would be a nice day, not too hot or chilly.

"Will you tell me more about your home?" she asked.

"That's just it," I said. "Is it my home?"

"You grew up there. You lived there until . . . See? I don't even know when you left the mountain."

"Two weeks ago."

"For the first time?"

"Yes." Before that, my father said there was too much

for me to do for our people, that I couldn't go to the surface. It was only when it was clear I was going to bolt that he relented to my request to join the team coming here to help negotiate more conditions in the treaty."

"Was it a big culture shock? From what I've read, the orc kingdom was built deep below the surface and in enormous caves. You have many cities and thousands of people."

"That's right."

"Is it dark there?"

"We have natural lighting, though it's not the same as the sun." I tipped my head back and soaked in the feeling of it shining on my face. I loved it here and never wanted to leave. "The first time I saw the sun, I pretty much gasped. Those around me who'd been here before laughed, though in a friendly way, telling me they'd done the same thing. The roofs of our caves are lined with tiny blue creatures that emit light intermittently, and it's pretty, though not the same. We have night like you do and what's similar to daytime, though it's not as bright as what you get from the sun."

"Are the lights insects like fireflies?"

"They're actually a plant. We foster them when we open a new area, carefully planting them in cracks in the stone. They live off the moisture in the air around us."

"That's incredible. Natural lights. Do you have electricity?"

"Something similar to hydroelectric, I believe you call it here, generated by rivers."

"I can't imagine living in a city built within an enormous underground cavern. Is it damp?"

I shrugged and finished my coffee. Cat quickly poured me some more from a carafe keeping it hot. "Sometimes it is, but our caves are so big that it doesn't feel the same as, say, when it rains here."

"It sounds amazing. You lived in the city, right?"

"Yes." In the castle. "My family has a large house."

"Ah, you live together. I'd moved out of Mom's house and into my own place before she died."

"It's common for orc families to share one big residence."

"You said your cousin lives with you. I assume it was just her and your parents?"

"Her parents died, and she moved in with us when she was ten. She's like a younger sister to me. I love Valina a lot."

"Is she much younger than you?"

We hadn't discussed ages. "I'm thirty and she's twenty-six."

"Four years is a lot when someone's ten and the other fourteen. I bet she followed you everywhere."

I smiled. "She's sweet and . . ." Our people loved her. I didn't want to mention that. Sometimes, the words to tell Cat who I truly was hovered on my tongue, but I held them back. What we had felt too new. Fragile.

I didn't want to ruin it by telling her I was the heir to the orc kingdom.

"She's an amazing person," I finished. I added cream

to my coffee, plus five spoons of sugar, something that shocked Cat when I first did it. Now she just smiled.

"I'm glad you were able to grow up close to her. I was an only child."

"I was lonely before Valina moved in with us, so I understand."

We sat, holding hands, watching people pass on the walkway beyond Cat's small fence. I planned to start scraping and painting it soon.

"Would you like to take a walk on the shore?" she asked. "There's public access not far from here. We can splash in the waves if you'd like."

"That sounds fun."

She opened her phone and frowned. "I was accepted into your fan club. You have over a hundred members already." Looking up at me with wide eyes, she shook her head. "They don't even know who you are. I think you're perfect, but how do they know that?"

I loved that she thought I was perfect, but I wasn't. I was just an orc trying to find his place in the world. "I don't understand any of this." They couldn't know who I was, or they'd announce it. "What are they saying about me?"

"Not much, just gushing about how cute you are, which they're totally right about. They're following all your posts."

"I've only made two." I'd found some photos of the diner online and shared them.

"That's nice of you to mention the diner."

"I hoped it would bring you more business. You deserve all the best in the world, and a lot of that comes from success."

"I didn't know your last name is Aerensten," she said. "I guess I should've looked closer at the paperwork you filled out when I hired you."

I nodded but said nothing. Aerensten was my mother's name before she took the royal name of my father. It wasn't a complete lie to use it since it was one of my five names.

"So far, they're just talking about how gorgeous you are and how they'd love to meet you," she said.

"I doubt they'll come here."

"Probably not."

She put her phone on the little table, and we left her house, walking toward the water. I'd seen the ocean a few times since I arrived, though in the Boston area where the treaty was being negotiated. It was much more crowded there than here.

"It's off-season, now," Cat said as we took off our shoes to *feel the sand between our toes.* "Most of the tourists have left. We'll see an influx of leaf peepers soon, and then some more tourists around Christmas, but for now, it's mostly locals."

We took a path meandering around mounds of soft sand with bits of green grass spurting from the tops and walked out into an open area with the ocean ahead and sand stretching forever on both sides.

Stopping, Cat sucked in a breath and released it.

"There's something wonderful about the smell, the sound of the waves, and the view that relaxes me completely. Whenever I come here, I leave feeling refreshed."

"It's incredible."

People walked along the shore or sat on blankets, locals or tourists. Houses had been built back from the water, and I could picture myself sitting on one of those decks.

Turning, I marveled at how breathtaking the ocean was.

Waves rushed up the shore and crested, dropping with a powerful force, their white foam creating a roar that echoed through the air. The ocean's deep blue hue caught my gaze and held it, pulling me forward. It seemed so vast, rising all the way to the sky. The water shimmered under the sunlight, each droplet like a precious jewel. As the wind tousled my hair, carrying with it a briny scent, the raw energy surrounded me.

"I see what you mean," I said with complete awe.

Cat squeezed my hand. She turned toward me and curled her finger, bringing my face down close to hers.

And when she kissed me, my shaky world righted itself all over again.

CHAPTER 9
CAT

Holding hands, we walked along the shore, the water teasing across our ankles before retreating.

I couldn't stop smiling at Deegar, watching as he took in the beauty of the ocean for the first time.

Eventually, we stopped and sat where the waves could creep close enough to kiss our toes.

"I've never seen anything like it," he said. "We have large lakes and wide rivers, but you can see the other side. The ocean appears to go on forever, though I know there are other bodies of land on the other side."

"The Earth's an amazing place, and I'm glad I get to share this tiny bit of it with you."

He tugged me onto his lap, and I leaned back against his chest with his arms around me. I'd never felt so complete.

"Mom and I used to come here all the time," I said.

"It's been rough since she died. We were close. I know some kids don't get along with their parents—"

"That sounds like me."

"I'm sorry. Mom and I were friends. We went out to dinner together on our days off and worked side by side each day. She carefully guided me, sharing the knowledge she'd gained through the years while never telling me what I should do. It takes a light touch to raise a child. You want to give them the freedom to make mistakes they can learn from, but you also want to keep them from being hurt."

"She sounds like a wonderful person."

I sniffed, my eyes stinging. I'd shed a lot of tears over the past year, and I'd mourn her forever, but it was nice to talk about her. "When I tell someone about her, I feel like a part of her still lives on. I wish everyone could've known her the way I did."

If only I could've introduced Deegar to her. She would've adored him as much as I did.

We'd only been together for a few days, but I felt like he and I had been friends forever, only parted. We'd reconnected and slipped back into where we left off. I sensed what we were building would last forever.

I shifted around to face him, taking in how his eyes sparkled in the sunlight and how the light breeze ruffled his dark hair.

We kissed, and I clung to his horns, savoring how amazing it felt just to touch him.

He ran his hands up and down my back, sending

tingles of electricity dancing through me. The warmth of his skin was like a balm to my soul. I felt safe, secure, and loved in his embrace.

His lips were soft against mine, his tusks firm. Everything inside me melted as I shifted in his arms. Could I imprint this moment on my mind to make it last forever?

Waves rippled along the shore, and the salty ocean breeze mixed with his spicy scent made my heartrate pulse. I felt more alive than I had before, and I'd do anything to hold on to this feeling. He deepened our kiss, and my moan rumbled in my throat.

We broke apart, and he cupped my face and stared into my eyes.

"You're precious to me," he said, his voice deep and growly.

Shivers tracked through me, and I wanted to take his hand and lead him back to my house. I wouldn't stop until we'd reached my bedroom, and I suspected once we started touching each other, we'd never leave the room.

People passing smiled our way as if sharing the happiness seeping from my pores. It felt good to be with someone special, someone I could trust.

I just hoped nothing stepped in to break us apart.

CHAPTER 10

DEEGAR

We had lunch at an open deck restaurant and walked lazily through town, holding hands. Stopping periodically, we gazed through store windows, Cat pointing out things she liked. We laughed softly together about things we both didn't enjoy, and I marveled at how our likes harmonized so completely.

Returning to her tidy home, we sat on the front porch again.

"Have you tried iced coffee?" she asked. "I happen to have brewed some this morning and put it in the fridge.

Grimacing, I shook my head. "Cold coffee? Who'd drink something like that?"

"Me." She smirked as she rose from her chair. "And you if you're brave enough to try it."

I followed her into the kitchen as she opened the refrigerator and pulled out a carafe. She set it on the counter and grabbed a couple of large glasses from the cupboard, adding ice and a bit of cream.

"We don't have cows in the orc kingdom."

"What?" she gasped. "Does that mean you don't have whipped or ice cream?"

I shook my head. "I've tried the latter. It's good. Sweet and cold on the tongue."

"Well, we've got to fix this immediately." With complete seriousness, she opened the fridge, returning the carafe, and pulling out a silver can. After popping the top, she held it toward me. "Close your eyes, open your mouth, and be prepared for an amazing treat."

"Being with you is the best treat in the world, Cat."

"Aw." Her mischievous smile widened. "But you haven't tried whipped cream yet."

I did as she asked, bending forward so she could reach.

A brief hissing-whooshing sound erupted as my mouth was filled with something light, fluffy, and sweet.

"Thoughts?" she asked, watching me.

I ran my tongue through the creamy, velvety treat. "Smooth," I mumbled around the bite. "Slightly sweet and luscious, like you, mate."

She grinned. "Ha."

I swallowed. "It has an airy quality that adds something I can't quite describe. It's quite delicious."

"We add it to coffee." She demonstrated by squirting some on the top of our beverages. "On pie or even cake, or just like this."

"What would it taste like . . ." Because my heat was brewing once more, my mind took me in a steamier direction.

"I think I know where you're taking this, *mate*." Placing the whipped cream on the counter, she turned back to me, her gaze focused on my cock jutting the cloth of my pants forward. "Would you mind giving me a taste?"

"I'm completely yours," I groaned.

She tugged down my pants and my erection sprang free. "You're amazing. So big and thick. I can't wait to give you a bite."

I chuckled, low and deep. "Don't bite too hard."

She squirted whipped cream on the head of my cock. "Now it's all dressed up." Leaning forward, she proceeded to lick the cream off, her tongue scratchy and unbelievably erotic.

The sensation was nearly overwhelming, and my guttural hiss rang out. My entire body heated up, my blood simmering in anticipation. She licked and sucked her way down the shaft, her tongue swirling around it as if she was savoring my flavor as much as that of the whipped cream. Her hands gripped my hips tightly, her nails digging into my skin.

Her mouth enveloped me, the movement of her lips and tongue sending waves of pleasure through my veins. With each stroke, I grew closer and closer to the edge until finally I could take no more and released everything I had with a roar that echoed off the walls.

She straightened with a satisfied smile, looking up at me with adoring eyes. "That was wonderful." Her grin widening, she wiped away a bit of the cream from the corner of her mouth and licked her finger. "You taste even better than whipped cream."

CHAPTER II

CAT

After that delightful break, I got back to the coffee. Deegar leaned against the counter, his gaze shooting from the can to my mouth over and over.

"I made it from cold brew, so it's really smooth and not too strong," I explained as I gave each glass a stir and added more cream on the top.

I handed him a glass, and he brought it to his nose, taking in the aroma before sipping.

"The flavor's unlike anything I'd ever had before—smooth yet slightly sweet, with an earthy undertone," he said. "It's amazing. What did you add? Spices?"

I shook my head. "Nope, it's just a touch of brown sugar and the whipped cream—the perfect combination for a fall day like this one."

We took our drinks outside to enjoy the last few moments of light before the sun slipped below the horizon. Snuggling together on the porch swing, we watched as the sky turned from vivid blue to deep orange and yellow.

Mosquitoes started to buzz around us.

"We don't have insects like this in the orc kingdom," he said, swatting one away.

"Let's go inside where they can't nibble." I couldn't stop thinking of what I'd done for him in the kitchen. The amazed look on his face. The way he'd bellowed when he came. The way he'd looked at me after, as if I meant everything to him.

Somewhere between the thrift shop and that can of whipped cream, I'd fallen in love.

What should I do about it?

I didn't have to think long or hard to come up with an idea.

We watched another romcom, him picking it out this time, laughing at the silly jokes and the cute way the couple fell in love. I felt like the characters' lives mirrored ours, and it wasn't hard to see us slipping into the same happy ending.

"Another day off tomorrow," I said. "What should we do?"

"We could walk on the beach again. It's amazing there. I can see why you love living so close."

"We could hike Trellor's peak if you'd like. It's only about three miles round trip, and the trail's easy. The view from the top can't be beat. The ocean stretches in front of you, dotted with islands, and if you use binoculars, you can see Canada in the distance."

"That sounds like the perfect way to spend the day." He rose, glancing at the clock. "I suppose we should go to bed now."

"Yup." I got up as well and walked toward my bedroom door.

"I'll try to wake before you do. I'd like to cook you breakfast."

"I adore bacon almost as much as you," I said with a sultry smile. "Though you're a close second."

His laugh barked out. "If you'd like, we could do a comparison in the morning."

"Or . . ." I gathered the courage to speak "Or . . . you could come to bed with me and give me a sample I can use when comparing to the bacon in the morning."

His eyes widened, but the sexiest smile crept across his face. "What are you offering, Cat?"

"Everything. Me. You. Any way you'd like to be with me."

"Are you sure?"

Nodding, I took a deep breath. "Yeah, I am. I want to be with you, Deegar."

"Mate," he breathed, striding toward me.

"I haven't been with anyone in what feels like forever," I croaked. "At least a year before Mom died. I was sad for such a long time. I couldn't bear to open myself up to someone new."

"I understand." He tugged me into his arms and held me. "I promise I won't hurt you."

Lifting me off my feet, he carried me into the bedroom.

CHAPTER 12

DEEGAR

I laid her gently on the bed and followed her down. My precious mate. I knew she had doubts about us. I'd been around humans long enough to know they didn't have the same faith orcs did about matings and fate.

But she was trusting me to show her how wonderful it could be between us. She may not know me much on the surface, but deep down, where it counted, she saw the true me. The person I'd only shown her.

I feathered my lips against hers, and when she cupped my shoulders and moaned, I pressed harder, claiming her mouth as I would her body. Her lips were soft and warm against mine, and my heart beat like the roll of thunder across the landscape. Anticipation made my throat tight. I wanted this moment to be perfect. I'd take my time, savoring every second. Yes, my cock was on fire. That was to be expected while I was in heat. But I needed her with me through everything we did.

I traced my fingers down her sides and slid them beneath her shirt, teasing across her soft belly. My pulse roared, and everything inside me told me to shred through her clothing. Claim her hard and fast. But it was vital I not hurt her. I was big, so much larger than her, and if I wasn't careful, this moment wouldn't be special.

Nudging up her shirt, I helped her remove it. Then the snug garment she wore beneath that restrained her glorious breasts. Piece by piece, I stripped her until she lay beneath me like a goddess. The fates had crafted her solely for me, and I was incredibly honored that she wanted to give herself to me.

"Tell me what feels good, what you like," I said, leaving her mouth to kiss down her neck, nibbling. Would she protest if I marked her as mine? I'd save that for later.

She tugged at my shirt, and like with her clothing, I wanted to rip through it. More than I craved the air, I needed to feel her skin against mine.

I marveled at how smooth her skin was, and the color, a light tan. So different from orc green.

Her hair was so lustrous, and I wanted to bury my face in it. I breathed in deeply, taking in her scent, and my heart filled with something bordering on love. I kissed her again, this time with more passion, and I felt her body respond to mine. She gripped my shoulders, her fingers warm on my skin.

I wanted to give her what she'd given me earlier with the whipped cream, and I'd grab the can tomorrow. Tonight, I'd show her complete joy. I wanted her to feel special, for her to know I was falling in love with her. I looked into her eyes and saw the same feeling shining from them. This moment was for both of us.

I moved lower, trailing my lips across her collarbone and down to her breasts. I wanted to savor every inch of her body. When I took one of her nipples in my mouth, she gasped and arched against me. Her hands threaded through my hair, urging me closer as I sucked and licked. My tongue traced circles around the tight peak before flicking it lightly.

"Yes, I like that. More." She moaned louder and stroked my horns. Fire shot from them to my cock, and it surged against my abs.

As she arched her back, pushing her breasts toward me, I smiled against her skin and continued exploring with my tongue until each of her nipples were hard peaks. My hands roamed up and down her body, feeling the curves of a woman made for me alone. The fates had been generous in giving me Cat, and I planned to treasure her always.

My heat was raging now, but I pushed it back with all my might. This moment was too precious to rush. Instead, I focused on giving her everything inside me, coaxing more moans from deep within her throat as I ran my fingers along her hips and thighs before sliding between them.

I kissed her inner thighs, and she shuddered beneath me.

"I want you, Deegar."

"And you shall have me, mate. Soon."

First, I needed another taste . . .

Her legs trembled as I moved closer to her heat. She was wet and ready for me, and I wanted to enjoy every second of this experience with her. I parted her folds with my tongue and licked upward until I came to her clit.

She clung to my horns as I sucked on her sweet pearl. Her hips rocked against me, pushing more of herself into my mouth as she moaned. She tasted like nectar, and I wanted to drink from her forever.

I slid two fingers inside her, pumping them while she gasped. Keeping up the rhythm with my tongue, I added a third finger, stretching her so she'd be able to handle my cock. The tremors in her body increased until I could tell she was near to coming undone.

Rising over her, I kissed her belly. Her mouth.

Her legs hitched around my hips as I centered my cock at her core.

With my gaze locked on hers, I pushed the thick head inside her.

CHAPTER 13
CAT

He pushed his hips toward me, and the head of his cock slid through my wetness and into the opening of my passage.

We both groaned at the heady sensation.

Holding his arms tight, I stared up at him, loving how gentle he was even in this.

"Love you," he whispered. "So much. I know it's too soon, too much, but I can't help telling you, mate." Pulling back, he drove forward again, seating himself deeper, though not all the way inside.

The stretch was intense, and I worried I wouldn't be able to take him all when I wanted to. All thought of speech flew from my mind.

He pulled back and thrust toward me again. This time, I bucked my hips up to meet him, and his cock sunk deeper.

"Mate," he growled. "You feel amazing. Can you take all of me, take my cock?"

"Show me," I growled right back at him. "Give it all to me. Make it fit."

"I don't want to hurt you."

"It doesn't hurt. It's tight." Incredibly tight. "But I want all of you."

"You're sure?"

I grinned. "Keep trying. Don't give up until you're buried to the hilt."

His gaze remained locked on me. "Your tight little pussy feels incredible. I'm going to give you more." He slipped from me and drove forward, harder this time. Sinking deeper.

I gasped as pleasure radiated through my body. It didn't hurt but damn was he huge. "I can take it." I could.

He grinned before it slipped from his face, replaced with an intensity that rocked me to my core. I could feel my body gushing, and when the nubs along the sides of his cock started vibrating, I whimpered.

He seated himself deeper with each thrust.

I moaned, caught up in the heady feeling. When the spur above his cock latched onto my clit and hummed, I cried out in joy. Soon we were both lost in a frenzied embrace. I ran my hands over his arms, savoring the flex of his muscles as he labored above me.

Love washed over me. He felt so good inside me—so powerful yet tender at the same time. It was all I could do not to give in and come this instant.

He pushed himself up, and I wrapped my legs around him. His thrusts grew more urgent, and I could feel him swelling within me, growing impossibly larger. Still, I took everything he had to give, and his groans of pleasure echoed around us.

His breath came in ragged gasps, and each time he thrust forward, his spur circled my clit, stroking it while vibrating.

I couldn't take much more, but I wanted this to last forever. Tension built inside me. I was a volcano about to blow, and I'd shoot all the way to the stars.

"Come for me, mate," he shouted. "You take my cock so well, so sweetly." He went faster, pistoning his hips to stroke every bit of my inner walls.

"Mate," he said, his voice low and raspy.

I grinned up at him, knowing he was close too.

"My glorious, wonderful mate. You're perfect. Feel how hard my cock is. I can't wait to let go. Give me your sweetness, love." He kept thrusting, faster and harder. His breathing was labored, and his eyes were shut tight as if to keep the heady feeling from overwhelming him.

My body gave way all at once, shudders rippling through me, bursting from my core.

With a bellow, he came as well, spilling his seed deep inside me.

CHAPTER 14

DEEGAR

"I probably should've told you earlier that I knot," I said, bracing myself over my lovely mate.

She grinned up at me. "For some reason, I'm picturing your cock coiling into a big twist inside me, but that can't be happening." Her head tilted, and her face scrunched. "Or is it?"

"The head of my cock is swelling, filling you."

"I think you filled me already," she said with a soft laugh. "I'm not sure there's any more room inside me for bulges."

"This locks my cock deep within you to give my seed a chance."

"I hate to break it to your seed, but I've got an IUD. Your seed can travel all it wants, but it's not going to find the same satisfaction as you."

"Would you ever want to have orclings?" I watched

her face. Perhaps this was something we should've discussed before we started, but the thought had flown from my mind. All I could focus on was pleasuring her and finding the same feeling within her body.

"I want kids, yeah," she said.

"Lots or just a few?" Still locked deep within her, I rolled with her in my arms, holding her close. If we could stay this way forever, I'd be a happy orc.

"I guess I'd let nature decide."

It wasn't hard to picture us together in a few years, our orclings running along the beach ahead of us, splashing through the waves. We could stay here in her cozy house or build something bigger right on the shore. Whatever she wanted.

Although, with a couple of orclings, we'd want more room than was available here.

But I was getting ahead of myself. I wanted to savor what we had now, which was each other.

"Your knot's getting bigger," she said. "Does it do that?"

"Actually, mate, my knot has gone down. My cock, however, is eager for another taste of your sweet pussy."

"I don't think we should deny your cock, do you?" She rolled to my side and then climbed over me, straddling my waist. Rising over me, she centered my cock at her opening and sunk down.

I slipped right inside her, and we both groaned.

My spur latched onto her clit, and she jolted, her

wide eyes meeting mine. The smile that teased across her lips made my heart clench tight. "You, my adorable orc, are quickly becoming addictive."

CHAPTER 15
CAT

When I woke, Deegar wasn't lying beside me. I sniffed the air, hoping to smell bacon or coffee, but no such luck.

"He needs more training," I said with a laugh. Although, when considering what we'd done in my bed the night before, he was already an expert. I'd been with guys in the past, but none of them had touched me as deeply as him. I wasn't teasing when I told him he was becoming addictive. I couldn't imagine moving forward in life without Deegar beside me.

"Hello?" I called out in the kitchen. And in the living room.

No Deegar.

I stuffed my feet into my slippers and grabbed my little-used robe from the closet and stepped out onto the front porch. He wasn't there either. Or in my tiny front yard or the area behind my house that was in sore need of mowing.

"Maybe he went to a coffee shop or . . . somewhere to pick up a treat to have with breakfast?"

I sunk into the porch swing where we'd snuggled and stared at the stars together, watching the street.

Two hours later, I was still there and getting worried.

After dressing, I made circles around the neighborhood. I went to the closed diner and even walked a mile or so in each direction on the beach.

By the time I returned home, I was sweaty and frantic. It only got worse when I found his phone lying on the kitchen counter. He wouldn't leave without it. I knew this in my heart.

I called the police, but they said it was too soon to fill out a missing person's report.

I fretted all afternoon and finally realized at about six that I'd eaten nothing all day.

I heated leftovers from the fridge and got teary while sitting on the front porch eating them.

At eleven, I made myself get ready for bed. The diner reopened in the morning, and it was beginning to look like I would be the sole server.

"Where are you, Deegar?" I whispered as I climbed under the covers. I hugged the pillow he'd slept on, sucking in his scent.

I didn't try to hold back my tears.

Two days later, I'd filed a missing person's report with the police and ran my tail off at the diner keeping up with business.

"Where's Deegar?" everyone asked. You'd think I hadn't worked here alone for the past year, that he was the only server.

"I hope he's back soon," Wilfred said with a frown.

So did I.

After work, I trudged home and slumped on the front porch—*not* sitting on the swing. That was where I'd fallen in love, and I didn't dare touch it.

"Where are you?" I asked softly, but there was no reply.

I scrolled through my phone, and it occurred to me to go to Chatbook, where I clicked into Deegar's fan page. Should I tell them he'd disappeared?

There was no need to say a thing . . .

. . . because he *hadn't* disappeared.

The group was full of recent shots of Deegar dressed in much fancier clothing.

Standing with his bodyguards at the embassy in Boston.

Dining with a gorgeous orc female at an exclusive restaurant.

Taking transport to the orc kingdom, a grim smile on his face as he waved to the crowd.

He was safe. He looked happy enough.

And he wasn't just plain old Deegar Aerensten. Nope,

he was actually *Prince* Deegar Aerensten Weelest Brilladon Tritemarden.

First in line for the throne of the orc kingdom.

He'd played me all along.

I threw my phone onto the side table, buried my face in my hands, and cried.

CHAPTER 16
DEEGAR

When I stepped outside Cat's house to collect her mail from the box, orcs rushed up to me. My bodyguards had found me.

I fought them using every bit of skill I possessed, but my family had hired them for a reason. They might be on my level as far as battle skills, but there was no way I could defeat five of them at once.

"Cat," I bellowed as they dragged me to their vehicle. "Cat!"

They stuffed me into the back of the enormous, armored truck and locked the doors, climbing into the front and engaging the inner armor we used if I was under threat. I couldn't escape. I couldn't bash my way through (though I tried), and they couldn't hear me try to convince them to let me go.

They drove until we reached the embassy.

That was when I realized I didn't have my phone. Fuck.

Carick, the head of my detail, lowered the privacy shield a crack and spoke through it. "You either come inside peacefully or you make a scene. As you can see, the press is here, greedy to record anything they can use against the orc kingdom and the royal family in general. What's it going to be, Prince Deegar?"

"I'll cooperate." For now.

My lips a thin line, I walked with them through the aisle created through the crowd with the press and people shouting all sorts of questions on both sides. They wanted to know where I'd been. What I'd done. And if this would have any impact on the treaty.

I said nothing, just kept my head held high and walked inside, where I was "guided" to one of the parlors where I was told to sit and remain in place.

Thankfully, the treaty negotiations had continued while I was away, following the guidelines I'd set forth that benefitted both humans and orcs alike. All that remained was for me to sign for the orc kingdom, which I promptly did.

"Give me your phone," I told Carick when I'd finished. I'd memorized Cat's number.

"I'm afraid I can't do that," he said grimly. We stood in the front parlor with my other bodyguards surrounding us like an orc wall. They were determined to keep me from running again.

"Why not?"

"I've been told to ensure you return to the kingdom after the treaty's signed."

"I fell in love. She's my true mate." Desperation filled my voice. I'd shout it to the world. I didn't care if anyone heard. "Please let me call her. She must be frantic, not knowing what happened to me."

For one second, sympathy crossed his face, but it was quickly replaced with resolution. "I can't. I'm sorry." His gaze flitted from mine. "We must leave now." Grabbing my arm, he and the others hustled me out the front door and through the press gauntlet again.

By then, I didn't care.

"Cat, I'm coming back to you," I bellowed.

"He has a new pet?" one of the press asked, and the rest snickered.

"I promise. I love you," I said as Carick stuffed me into the back of the armored vehicle.

More laughter erupted outside, but I didn't care. All I could do was pray to the fates she got my message.

CHAPTER 17
CAT

Three days later, I was working in the diner when a commotion erupted outside. Lights flashed as if a storm was approaching, though the day was clear and sunny.

The front door burst open and Deegar—no, make that *Prince* Deegar—strode inside. His gaze snapped around the diner before pinning me in place where I stood behind the bar, a carafe of coffee in my hand.

"Hey," Dr. Yang said. "Hey!"

Everyone stopped speaking. Some turned toward the door while others looked at me.

I realized I'd not only filled Dr. Yang's coffee cup but the saucer beneath.

"Sorry," I mumbled, dropping the carafe on the counter beside his cup.

"Cat," Deegar said softly. "Cat."

How could I face him after he'd held back the most important part of himself?

I spun on my heel and bolted through the kitchen and out the back door. I rushed through the neighbor's backyard and when I hit the street, I veered toward the ocean, not stopping until I stood so close to the water, the waves splashed on my work sneakers.

I couldn't see a damn thing; my eyes kept weeping. The tears trickled down my cheeks and plopped in the sand by my feet.

"Cat," Deegar said, coming up behind me. "I'm sorry. I hoped you'd be happy to see me."

I was. More than anything.

"You left," I said, bitterness filling my mouth. "You never sent word. I was scared something had happened to you." At first that is. "Then I went to your fan page and . . ."

"You found out who I am."

"Yeah."

He walked around to my front, splashing through the water, facing me. He seemed oblivious to the waves smacking against the backs of his legs. "I love you."

"My heart's shattered. I spent the past five days worrying that you were dead. I filed a police report, and let me tell you, I felt foolish after I went to your fan page and saw pictures of you having fun signing a treaty, savoring a dinner with a gorgeous orc woman, and returning to the orc kingdom as if everything we said to each other, everything we did, meant nothing."

He took my hands and dropped to his knees. "I went to collect your mail, and my bodyguards grabbed me."

That would explain why he didn't have his phone.

"They tracked me down after my posts about the diner on Chatbook." He clung to my hands when I tried to pull away. "I fought them, but there were too many of them and they were chosen because they're the best the kingdom has to offer. My family has an armored vehicle. I couldn't escape to come back to you."

"Because of the treaty signing?" I'd read about it online.

"I was told it was ready and if I didn't sign, the deal wouldn't go through. I love you. I want to be with you. I would've endangered everything to come back to you, but I couldn't break free."

"What about the orc woman?"

He frowned and shook his head. "I don't know who you mean." When his face cleared, he sighed. "If you saw pictures of me with . . ." He pulled his wallet from his back pocket—a very humanlike thing that surprised me —and slipped out a photo of the same woman. "This is my cousin, Valina."

"She's pretty."

"She's amazing." He grinned, though it held too much sadness. "She's now the heir to the orc kingdom. I've renounced the throne and handed it to her."

"You didn't," I breathed.

"I did." He flashed me a smile, but it faded fast. "I'm sorry I didn't tell you who I am. I should've. But . . . It's stupid actually, but at first, I wanted to be a regular old orc, someone who'd walk into a diner and meet the woman of his dreams. And then as I got to know you, I wasn't sure how to tell you. I can't make that up to you, but if you give me a second chance, I'll try."

"Deegar." I wasn't sure what to say. I'd tried to stamp out the love I felt for him, but it was impossible. "You really gave up the throne?"

He nodded. "I spent the past three days in the orc kingdom fixing this so I could return to you and be with you always. Didn't you see my message on TV?"

I shrugged. "I haven't watched TV."

"Not even a romcom?"

How could I when he wasn't sitting beside me, laughing? "No."

"Do you have your phone handy?"

"Why?"

He held out his hand. "I don't have mine, so I can't show you."

No harm in that. I handed it over and he scrolled it with a skill I envied.

"When did you get so good with phones?" I asked.

"I made my head bodyguard show me how to use it while we waited for the final treaty paperwork and as he took me back to the orc kingdom." He turned the phone my way. "Note the date."

Three days ago.

He pressed play on the video, and it showed him

leaving the embassy, shouting out for me and telling me he loved me, that he'd come back to me.

I tried to swallow, but it wouldn't pass the solid lump in my throat. "I didn't see it."

"I made a vow, and I've kept it. I'm here. I want to stay with you forever. And I love you more than life itself. What do you say? Will you be my true mate, my forever love, and the reason I exist?"

My heart split wide open and the pain I'd felt for days spilled out. No, it was pushed out by my love for this orc.

"I love you, Deegar," I croaked. "I missed you so much."

He opened his arms. "That's all I needed to hear."

I jumped into his arms, and he spun me around while we kissed. He lost his footing and tumbled into the water, shocking us both.

We rolled in the water, still kissing.

And there wasn't anything better than that.

CHAPTER 18

EPILOGUE
CAT

One Year Later

"Here she is," Deegar said softly. "Hungry and determined to be with her mama." He laid our one-month-old daughter in my arms, and she whimpered, rooting against my chest. He'd heard her first and jumped from the bed, going to her room to change her diaper and bring her to me before I could roll over.

As I fed her, he dropped onto the bed beside me, his arm going around my shoulders. He stroked the smooth green skin on her forehead and teased his fingertip across her newly formed tiny horns. She looked so much like him it made my heart flip each time I saw her.

He kissed my cheek and twirled my hair around his finger. "Feeling alright?"

"Perfect." I turned my face, and we kissed deeply.

"I think everything's packed and ready for the movers."

He'd made sure it was, diligently tucking all our belongings carefully into boxes. The movers would be here tomorrow. Or today, I guessed, since it was after midnight.

"I still can't believe we'll have an oceanfront home," I said. "I love it, but I'll be sad to say goodbye to Mom's place." It was too small. We were going to rent it to tourists during the summer and a local person for the winter.

"We'll still be able to take care of it. We could even spend a night there ourselves every now and then."

Which would be fun. Memories and all that.

We got married not long after he tracked me down on the beach. It was a small ceremony. We didn't want the press or anyone there but our friends. His parents couldn't come, but Valina did and she grinned during the entire ceremony.

We'd hired staff to work at the diner, freeing me to do managerial duties.

Then we closed the diner for two weeks (paying everyone to take a vacation) and went to the orc kingdom for our honeymoon. Of course, we stopped to see Valina happily learning the duties that would be expected of her when she took over the throne from Deegar's father.

"Mom and Dad will be here next week to meet

Nunnea. My mom won't put her down." He grinned at our daughter with so much love, it made my throat tighten.

We stopped by the castle during our honeymoon. His parents were stern at first, angry that he'd given up the throne and blaming me. But they soon warmed up, and by the time we left, they gave us each bittersweet hugs. They were calling me daughter by then, and they understood why he didn't wish to rule.

"I hope this time, they don't let the press know they're here," I said. I wasn't the kind who enjoyed being in the spotlight any more than Deegar. We'd remained hidden, our neighbors and friends doing their best to keep the press out of our lives.

His parents had come to visit twice, and this little town had never seen anything like it, though they got used to seeing bodyguards and the press around. Thankfully, things returned to normal after they were gone.

"We'll have to scurry to unpack everything at the new house to be ready before they arrive to stay with us," I said.

"It'll be amazing. I've hired extra crew to help. Even Marge and Dr. Yang are coming by to either babysit or help us unpack. We'll be ready before they get here."

That was good because there was so much stuff! How did I collect it all inside that tiny house?

Now we'd have three bedrooms and an office. A huge deck overlooking the ocean. A gorgeous kitchen. And a master suite with a tub big enough for two orcs—or in this case, him and me.

Actually, I couldn't wait to move in.

Mom would understand why I no longer lived in the place I grew up in. She'd want the best for me, and she'd be proud of how my life had turned out.

And she'd be thrilled to see me happy with Deegar.

Catch up with Deegar and Cat
in the Love at First Orc Series.

Shh... Cat will so be pregnant, and you'll get
to meet their new orcling!

The Love at First Orc Series

Orc-us Pocus
Orc-ishly Ever After
Tinsel & Tusks
Orc Charming
Gaming the Orc
Orc-wardly Yours

Companion stories
Single Orc Dad
(part of the Sweet Monster Treats world)

Scroll forward to read Chapter 1 of Gaming the Orc . . .

ORC-US POCUS

An orc science teacher is determined to give me a lesson in chemical reactions.

I've crushed on my fellow high school teacher, Thraal, since we first met up in the staff lounge. He's a big, brawny orc, and when he scowls at me through his thick glasses, I pretty much ignite. Sadly, he doesn't realize I exist.

When we're trapped inside the janitor's closet during a Halloween dance, I take the opportunity to show him I'm special. A few spontaneous kisses suggest he might like me too.

Until we're rescued, and he goes back to ignoring me. Well, other than when we get stuck beneath the bleachers or when we're locked inside the field hockey supply shed overnight.

Can I find true love with a geeky orc science teacher?

Orc-us Pocus is a spicy monster romcom and Book 1 in the Love at First Orc Series. Each book is standalone but expect cameos.

Expect size difference, plenty of spice, falling for a co-worker, an awkward, geeky, glasses-wearing orc who loves science and has a creative tongue, laugh out loud moments, fated mates in heat, and a happy ever after.

Love at First Orc Series
Orc-us Pocus
Orc-ishly Ever After
Tinsel & Tusks
Orc Charming
Gaming the Orc
Orc-wardly Yours

Companion Stories
Single Orc Dad

CHAPTER 1
AUTUMN

I stood along the wall in the high school gym, doing my best to chaperone the Halloween dance, but mostly checking out the muscular ass of our high school science teacher, Thraal.

A few years ago, orc males marched out of a previously unknown tunnel on the side of a huge mountain and announced they were seeking mates.

Humans said, okay, sure, we'll give it a try. Treaties were formed, and they now lived among us.

Thraal took a job as the high school's science teacher and started after Labor Day.

"He's so cute," I sighed to my best friend and fellow teacher, Kassia.

Kassia stabbed her finger toward two kids on the dance floor. "Hey, no making out. Megan? Sam? Stop it!" She huffed, sending strands of her strawberry blonde hair shooting up from her forehead. She turned to me. "*Who's* so cute? Because there are a couple of options."

She and I had shared a room in college, graduating with our education degrees seven years ago, and because we were besties, we'd applied to the same school district. Thankfully, Baneroot Academy hired us both.

Kassia taught social studies and world government classes, and I taught math, plus oversaw the Math Club.

"Thraal," I breathed. Per usual, he had a flock of groupies clustered around him, a mix of single teachers and a few students. Also, per usual, he didn't appear to notice their attention. Unfailingly polite and formal (except for his outfit tonight), he appeared oblivious to everyone around him. His steely black eyes scrutinized the room through his Clark Kent glasses.

He was the sweetest guy, completely opposite from my controlling ex.

"You've got it bad," Kassia said.

"Yeah," I said. "Would it be crass to go over and ask him if he's dressed in ceremonial clothing or if the sorta Viking outfit is a costume?"

"Do it," Kassia said, punctuating her words with a nudge of her elbow into my side. She'd dressed as a fairy, complete with sheer wings and a glittery ballerina skirt and bodysuit, and frankly, she looked amazing. Why Jarum, an orc she was crushing on, didn't notice was beyond me.

"I don't know if I dare," I said with a cringe.

"Do it!"

Her low laughter followed me as I started forward, the tulle skirt of my black witch skirt swishing across my fishnet stockings, trying to hold my head steady so my tall, pointed black hat wouldn't slide off my head.

I turned back and scurried over to her, my heels clicking on the wooden gym floor.

"What should I say?" I asked, my voice high pitched and thready.

"Start with hello?" Her gaze locked on Jarum, the school's orc Phys Ed teacher.

"Ya think?" I said with a wry twist of my lips. "It's what comes after hello that I seem to have a problem with."

"You should've stomped over to Wanda and hip-checked her away from him at lunch the other day. Then you'd be past hello already."

I'd started toward him, determined to sit with him while we ate. Talk with him. Adore him from up close. Only to have another teacher claim his attention with a sly smirk sent my way.

"If I fumble my words, he's going to think I've got a problem with social skills," I said. "Give me some tips, oh sophisticated one."

"If I had great social skills, I'd be chatting up Jarum right now."

"Let's make a pact," I said. "I'll go over to Thraal and offer to cast a spell on him." I lifted my witchy wand to punctuate my words. "And you go ask Jarum to dance."

"We're chaperoning. We're not allowed to dance."

"You can help him hold up the wall." He was leaning just like her.

"Alright, it's a deal," she said, nudging me toward Thraal. "Go on. He won't hurt you."

Unlike my controlling ex who'd thankfully had moved to a new town and was leaving me alone.

As I skittered along the outside of the big open gym, lights ricocheted off the disco balls hanging from the rafters, and orange and black streamers fluttered in the sweltering air. The summer heat had held for weeks, and we were all praying for a break. Thunder clouds rumbled on the horizon, but so far, the promise of a heavy rain—and cooler air—hadn't arrived.

Because I knew I'd chicken out if I thought too hard about it, I half-ran over to Thraal. Stopping a few feet away, I swallowed to hold back my sigh of adoration.

The coarse fabric of his dark blue vest shifted, giving me peeks of his medium-green skin. His abs went on for miles, a rugged terrain I'd kill to explore. The intricate gold embroidery on the front of his vest glowed and the fur trim gave his costume a claim-me-now warrior feel.

A leather belt encircled his waist, adorned with silver stars and strapped with both a blunted silver sword and short blade. He wore fur boots and a metal helmet, with the thick golden horns jutting out at his temples.

"Just carry me away and ravish me now," I whispered, my fingers twitching.

His gaze sought mine. Shit, had he heard me? From

the way his eyes smoldered as they traveled down my curvy frame, I suspected he had.

Before I could spin and hide my overheated face, he stomped toward me.

"You're in charge of clean-up, aren't you?" he asked in a neutral voice.

So much for thinking he might be eager to ravish me.

"Yeah, why?" I asked.

"Someone spilled punch all over the floor."

"We could call the janitor."

He scowled, never a good sign. "She's not on call, which means you, assigned clean-up, will have to take care of this."

"Okay. I'll get a mop. And a bucket. Water. And anything else I can find in the janitor's closet."

"I'll go with you."

I twisted my lips. "Do you think I'm going to ignore this?"

"I didn't say that."

"No, but you implied it."

He frowned, creating creases on his heavy orc brow. "I'm going with you because you're a tiny human."

"I'm tougher than I look." I lifted my arm and made a fist, but I lost some kick while holding a witch's wand.

Grunting, he crossed his arms over his sizeable chest. "Do you want my help or don't you?"

"I'd be foolish to turn down such a delightful offer."

He grunted again.

"This way." I passed him, aiming for the other side of

the gym. There were janitorial closets all over the high school, but the closest one would be inside the locker room.

He followed me to the door and inside, where we passed rows of lockers and approached the door to the closet in the back.

"Inside here," I said, holding up the master key I was given by the principal this afternoon—with a warning not to lose it.

I unlocked the door and stepped inside the tiny room.

Thraal followed, the door shutting behind him.

Three steps took me to the sink where the janitor had left a bucket. Mops and various housecleaning tools hung from hooks on both walls. I turned on the water, added a few squirts of a solution sitting on a shelf, and grabbed a mop, plopping the rag head inside the foaming water.

Thraal hovered behind me. If I stepped backward, I'd brush against him. The thought of pressing myself against his muscular frame made me close my eyes. I sunk into the dream where I rubbed my butt against his rising cock, his arms eagerly wrapping around me. His hands cupped my breasts and—

"Why are you moaning as if you're wounded?" he asked, his voice low and raspy in my ear. Reaching around me, he turned off the water.

While I was lost in Thraal-land, the bucket had filled. Water sloshed over the lip.

"You're not paying attention," he said in a gruff, grumbly voice.

"Are you always this impatient?" The words popped out of me.

He just chuckled, the husky sound tickling down my spine. "What makes you think I am?"

I turned to face him, my boobs brushing against his upper abs. He was so much taller than me. My five-six to his seven-feet put my lips at nipple height.

His abs twitched, and a vein throbbed in his chiseled temple. Tusks jutted from his lower jawline, and from the moment I met him, I'd wondered what it would be like to kiss his full, dark green lips, to run my tongue along his tusks. I'd grasp his horns and hold on while he . . .

He grunted. "Why do you smell aroused?"

Get Orc-us Pocus Now!

9 798869 108944